LIFE WITH A LEARNING DISORDER

BY JAMES BOW

Published by The Child's World®
1980 Lookout Drive • Mankato, MN 56003-1705
800-599-READ • www.childsworld.com

Content Consultant: Elizabeth Swanson, Ph.D., Research Associate Professor, The College of Education, The University of Texas at Austin

Photographs ©: Michael Jung/Shutterstock Images, cover, 1; Shutterstock Images, 6, 14, 16; Light Field Studios/iStockphoto, 8; iStockphoto, 11, 19, 20; Babirad Picture/Rex Features/AP Images, 12

ISBN 9781503825154
LCCN 2017959675

Printed in the United States of America
PA02375

TABLE OF CONTENTS

FAST FACTS

- A learning disorder is a problem in the brain that affects someone's ability to remember, learn, or communicate information. The brain makes connections differently, so someone with a learning disorder has difficulty processing certain kinds of information.
- There are three main types of learning disorders: dyslexia, dyscalculia, and dysgraphia. People with dyslexia have trouble reading and processing language. People with dyscalculia have trouble with math and numbers. People with dysgraphia have trouble writing words.
- Approximately 2.4 million US schoolchildren deal with learning disorders each year.
- It is not known exactly what causes learning disorders. Some experts think they run in families. Sometimes, learning disorders develop after a head injury. They may also be caused by a lack of **nutrition** when a child is very young or by exposure to **toxic** substances, such as lead.
- There is no cure for learning disorders, but they can be treated. **Tutors** and special education services can help children perform better in school.

SPECIAL EDUCATION

Special education can help people with learning disorders find new and effective ways to learn. The graph below shows the percentage of special education students between the ages of six and 21 in the United States who have learning disorders.

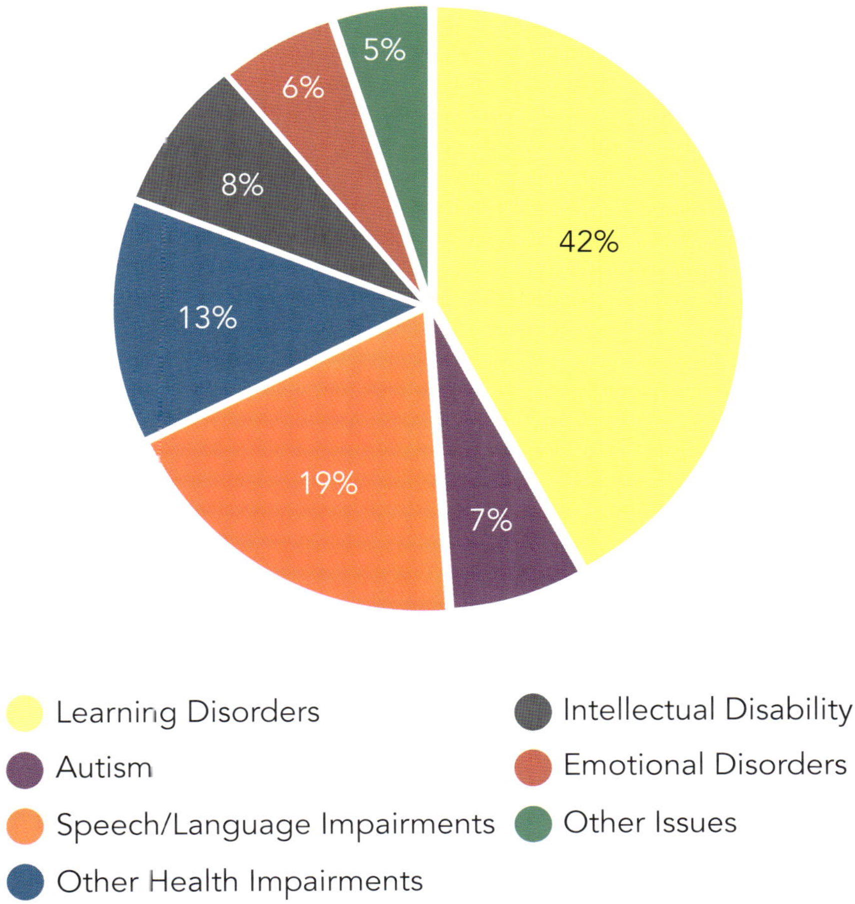

Chapter 1

SARAH'S NIGHT OUT

Sarah shifted on her feet outside the movie theater. She wondered if she had accidentally shown up early. She looked at the time on her phone, but the numbers weren't making any sense. The doors to the theater were locked, and people inside were setting up. She smiled. That meant she was early. It was better to be early than to be late.

Though she was great at reading and writing, Sarah always had trouble with numbers. Two years ago, in third grade, she had frozen in fear whenever her math teacher gave the class quizzes. She had not been able to complete many of the quizzes in the time given.

◄ **Learning to read and remember numbers is challenging for people who have dyscalculia.**

▲ **Tutors can help people with dyscalculia learn special skills that will help them with math.**

Sarah worked hard on all of her math assignments. But she kept getting poor grades. Her parents were concerned. They took Sarah to the school **counselor**.

The counselor gave Sarah a test. Sarah felt nervous at first. She didn't like tests. But the counselor said it wasn't like a school test. It was a math **fluency** test. It would determine her mathematical abilities so that the school would know the best methods to help her learn math. It wasn't a test she could fail.

After the test, Sarah's counselor told her parents that Sarah had dyscalculia. Sarah learned why she found math to be difficult.

DIAGNOSIS

Once parents and teachers understand that a child struggles in school, they will want more information about the child's reading, mathematical, or writing abilities. The child's parents or guardians may take him or her to see a counselor outside of school. Another option is to see a school counselor. Either way, the child will be asked to take several tests that ask many questions. The child's answers to these questions will help identify his or her strengths and areas of need.

Sarah's brain had a hard time processing numbers. Her math teacher promised to give her extra time and teach her different ways to learn math.

Sarah looked up as her friends arrived. Together, they headed over to the box office as it opened to buy their movie tickets. Sarah looked up at the showtimes, picked the movie her friends had chosen, and took out her purse to pay.

Counting money was another kind of test for her. It was hard for Sarah to remember which bills to hand over and how to count the change. But she took her time. Her friends waited patiently, not rushing her.

The cashier handed Sarah her ticket and the correct change. Sarah felt a sense of accomplishment as she and her friends walked into the theater.

People with dyscalculia may have a hard time counting or adding money. ▶

JAMIES
SUPERFOOD
für jeden Tag

Chapter 2

CHEF JAMIE OLIVER

Jamie Oliver first finished reading a book when he was 38 years old. The British chef and restaurant owner loves disappearing into a good story. But his dyslexia makes it difficult for him to focus and finish reading books. Still, Jamie has always enjoyed hard work and taking on cha lenges.

As a young boy, Jamie struggled in school. When he tried to read, he had trouble arranging letters into words. He was placed in a different classroom than his friends to receive extra help with reading. His teachers were supportive, but Jamie sometimes felt they didn't understand his dyslexia. Some classmates teased him.

◄ **Jamie Oliver has written more than 20 books about cooking and food.**

▲ **Jamie's goal is to create healthy and delicious recipes.**

But Jamie knew he had other talents. He loved cooking. He helped out in the kitchen at his parents' restaurant. He started exploring new ways to cook.

At the age of 16, Jamie went to Westminster Kingsway College in London, England, to study **home economics**. He later started working as a chef. Then, in 1997, Jamie appeared in a documentary.

The film was about the café where he was working. The BBC television network gave him his own show later that same year.

Jamie says dyslexia helped him become who he is. He looked for things he was good at and enjoyed doing, and he followed those passions. Today, he campaigns for better school meal programs and is one of the top bestselling British authors.

DEFINING DYSLEXIA

Dyslexia is the most common learning disorder. Approximately 80 percent of people with learning disorders have dyslexia. In addition to affecting a person's reading abilities, dyslexia may affect a person's writing abilities. It may be difficult for the person to spell or sound out words. A dyslexic person's brain processes language differently than a non-dyslexic person's brain. It is often difficult for someone with dyslexia to translate language into thought or thought into language. Tools such as audiobooks and software that reads text aloud can help.

Chapter 3

JAKE'S ASSIGNMENT

Twelve-year-old Jake looked up as the bell rang, announcing the end of English class. The teacher passed out worksheets for tomorrow's homework. Jake looked over the assignment. There were fill-in-the-blank spaces for him to write his answers. Jake pulled out his portable tablet computer. He took a picture of the worksheet. He uploaded it to an **app**. The app would help him complete the assignment.

When Jake got home from school, he started on his English homework first. He tapped the screen on his tablet to open the app. The worksheet filled the screen. He read through the first question on the sheet.

◀ **People with dysgraphia have difficulties with writing.**

Jake tapped on the fill-in-the-blank space. He used his index finger to write in the answer.

Jake had a type of learning disorder called dysgraphia. This disorder made it difficult for him to write. He could understand and easily repeat back information he had learned. But when it came to writing words by hand, he struggled. His handwriting was often unreadable and full of mistakes, no matter how hard he tried.

A few years ago, Jake would have been terrified by any tasks that required him to write things by hand. His parents had then taken him to see the school counselor. She had given him tests on his handwriting, spelling, and grammar. Those tests helped them find out that Jake had dysgraphia.

Special tools such as apps helped Jake to adapt. He also had regular visits with an **occupational therapist**. She showed him ways to practice writing by hand.

Tools such as tablet apps can help students with dysgraphia succeed in school. ▶

▲ **Some people with dysgraphia use lines or grids to help guide them when they write.**

Jake sometimes used a slant board to help him write. This tool provided a slanted surface. He could clip sheets of paper onto the board. Writing at an angle allowed him to extend his fingers into a more natural writing position. This kept him from getting cramps in his wrist and hand when he wrote.

Jake's teachers were also understanding. They let him take notes on his tablet. They gave him more time to finish handwritten tests. He also had the option of one-on-one tests in which a teacher asked him the questions, and he responded aloud.

Jake still didn't understand everything about his dysgraphia. But he knew his handwriting was slowly improving. He believed his hard work would keep paying off, one homework assignment at a time.

THINK ABOUT IT

- How might a learning disorder affect different aspects of a person's life?
- Think of your favorite hobby or activity. How might you adapt it for someone who has a learning disorder?
- How could you be a good friend to someone who has a learning disorder?

GLOSSARY

app (AP): An app is an application on a mobile device that performs a special function. Jake used an app to help complete a homework assignment.

counselor (KOWN-suh-lur): A counselor is an expert who is trained to give advice to help people manage disorders and health conditions. A school counselor helped Sarah discover that she had dyscalculia.

fluency (FLOO-en-see): Fluency is the ability to remember and apply certain information. The math fluency test Sarah took assessed her mathematical ability.

home economics (HOHM ek-uh-NOM-iks): Home economics is the study of cooking and other practical skills that are useful in maintaining a home. In college, Jamie Oliver studied home economics.

nutrition (noo-TRISH-uhn): Nutrition is the substances in food that your body needs to stay healthy. A lack of nutrition may cause learning disorders in young children.

occupational therapist (ok-yuh-PAY-shuhn-uhl THAIR-uh-puhst): An occupational therapist is a person who helps people develop skills in certain activities. Jake had an occupational therapist to help him develop skills to improve his handwriting.

toxic (TOK-sik): Something that is toxic is bad or harmful. Exposure to toxic substances, such as lead, may cause learning disorders.

tutors (TOO-torz): Tutors are teachers who often specialize in certain subjects and are trained to educate people who have trouble learning in traditional environments. Children with learning disorders often have tutors to help them learn.

TO LEARN MORE

Books

Cummings, Rhoda Woods. *The Survival Guide for Kids with LD.* Golden Valley, MN: Free Spirit, 2016.

Silverstein, Alvin, Virginia Silverstein, and Laura Silverstein Nunn. *Handy Health Guide to Dyslexia.* Berkeley Heights, NJ: Enslow, 2014.

Squire, Ann. *Dyslexia.* New York, NY: Children's Press, 2017.

Web Sites

Visit our Web site for links about learning disorders:
childsworld.com/links

Note to Parents, Teachers, and Librarians: We routinely verify our Web links to make sure they are safe and active sites. So encourage your readers to check them out!

SELECTED BIBLIOGRAPHY

Cortiella, Candace, and Sheldon H. Horowitz. *The State of Learning Disabilities: Facts, Trends and Emerging Issues.* New York, NY: National Center for Learning Disabilities, 2014.

Herschkowitz, Norbert, and Elinore Chapman Herschkowitz. *A Good Start in Life: Understanding Your Child's Brain and Behavior from Birth to Age 6.* New York, NY: Dana Press, 2004.

"Learning and Attention Issues." *Understood.org.* National Center for Learning Disabilities, n.d. Web. 4 Dec. 2017.

INDEX

ABOUT THE AUTHOR

James Bow is the author of more than 40 nonfiction books for children. He is a graduate of the University of Waterloo in Ontario, Canada, and is a freelance writer and editor. He currently lives outside Toronto, Canada, with his wife and two daughters.